I0829670

HQH₂O

HIGH QUALITY H₂O

SHEFFTAL A. BAILLOU II

BALOWZOOM
BOOKS

TABLE OF CONTENTS

HQH$_2$O High Quality H$_2$O

bzoombooks.com

BALOWZOOM BOOKS

Produced and Printed in the USA

The 8th and 13th pages in physical books are intentionally left blank as a nuanced homage to my roots in Tampa, represented by the 813-area code. These empty pages symbolize the power of presence and silence. The spaces where creativity, reflection, and meaning are born. Just as my city shaped me, these pauses in the book allow readers to shape their own thoughts and interpretations, making the journey uniquely personal. It's my quiet signature, a tribute, and an invitation all at once.

FOR THOSE WHO HOLD THESE PAGES

This book is more than a collection of words. This book is a labor of love, reflection, and devotion to the timeless art of poetry. Every line was written with intention, every page crafted to resonate deeply with the heart and soul. This is not a fleeting trend or a shallow attempt to capitalize on a moment. It is my sincere offering to the world. HQH2O is a celebration of language, emotion, and the power of human connection.

My hope is that these poems and the guidance provided will inspire you to embrace the beauty of meaningful expression. This is a work meant to stand the test of time, offering something unique to each reader, whether you return to it in days or years to come.

Thank you for taking the time to explore these pages. May they bring you joy, understanding, and the courage to use words with love and purpose.

With gratitude,
Shefftal A. Baillou II

INTRODUCTION

Attention from the one you love is one of the most phenomenal feelings in the world. In my life, I've found that setting yourself apart from other competitors can give you a slight edge. This short poetry read gives the reader the opportunity to do just that. By using kind words and occasional nice actions, you can manage to conquer even the most challenging levels of the game. Love is not a priority for everyone. Some people have been so damaged by past experiences that love is no longer the goal. By loving the wrong souls, I too have experienced pain so deep that it felt like a part of me was irreparably destroyed, like an unforgettable dark cloud in my soul that remained long after my tears had dried. How you react to the pain is what will either make you or break you. Not everyone is so blessed to find love again once betrayal and lies block your divine vision. Our minds may become occupied with thoughts of retaliation, deception, and getting the last laugh. My advice is to take time for yourself. Spoil yourself, spoil others, love yourself while attempting to love others, reflect on your actions, and meditate on your thoughts often. Through these actions, you will find inner peace and answers to the questions you once thought undiscoverable.

I once read that with the first breath of the infant begins the race to the grave. In the marathon of life, it's important to stretch, extend your reach, and touch others' lives' in the most unexpected and amazing ways. It's also important to reserve your energy; everyone is simply not worthy, and you will need it in the long run. Remember to stay hydrated; it's important to ingest the highest quality H2O that you are blessed to discover.

DEDICATION

Water is essential to all living forms of life. Water hydrated me when life dried me out. Water baptized my soul. Water detoxified and flushed toxins away. Water eroded and dissolved the scar tissue left behind from previous trauma. Water regulated my body temperature and made sweltering feel like a cool breeze. Water helped me digest the cleverest food for thought. Water felt my vibrations, and like a ripple effect, water began giving me higher frequencies more frequently. Water is strong, water is calm, water is pure. Water gave me strength to endure. Water cured me. Water replenished my insatiable thirst and continued to pour until my cup runneth over. Water fixed my smile like a dentist. Water's inspiration is endless. Water made me relentless. Water warmed my spirit and thawed my heart from a glacier. Water is a woman's daughter—call her mother Nature.

How to Use This Book to Ignite Romance: A Step-by-Step Guide

Welcome to your secret weapon for winning hearts. This collection of 35 heartfelt poems is designed to help you express your deepest feelings in the most unique and captivating way. Follow these instructions and watch as your love interest becomes drawn to your sincerity and creativity.

1. Establish the Foundation:

(Recommendation) Inform the intended recipient of the poetry that their beauty, brains, spirit etc..... inspires you to be creative. This way you don't come off as weird. It's a new era in dating. Most people aren't used to receiving heartfelt POETRY. This warning can build anticipation for the Recipient.

Pick a time when you know your love interest will be able to focus on your message. Whether it's morning, lunch, or evening, consistency is key.

2. Ease into it:

Begin with the softer, less personal poems. These will set a warm tone without being overwhelming. Think of this as planting the first seeds of intrigue.

3. One Poem Per Day:

Patience is your ally. Send one poem daily for 30 days—whether by text, handwritten note, or read aloud. Keep it steady and avoid skipping days to maintain momentum.

4. Personalize It:

After a few days, tailor your delivery. Add a personal touch like referencing an inside joke or a shared memory to deepen the connection.

5. Build to a Crescendo:

As the days progress, escalate the intensity. Use the more passionate poems to mirror your growing feelings. Let the rhythm of the words convey what's in your heart.

6. Keep It Authentic:

Your love interest will sense sincerity. Use these poems as a foundation but let your own feelings shine through.

By the end of the month, you'll have spoken a love language so compelling, it will be impossible to ignore. Take a chance, and let poetry open the doors to their heart.

HAVE FUN WITH IT!! MIX AND MATCH TO FIT YOUR SCENARIO! This book is for Self-Empowerment purposes. Energy can't be destroyed, only transferred. When you give positive energy to someone, the return may surprise you! Be Blessed, not Stressed!!!

HQH$_2$O

HIGH QUALITY H$_2$O

VOLUME I

BALOWZOOM BOOKS

I think the saying goes: out of sight out of mind.

But even out my sight, I can't get you off of mines.

With actions and my words Love, I'll try to redefine.

With such a speedy mind, I know you'll read between the lines.

It's care in every line, and Love in every word.

Because when God made you, he made something so superb!

I Love You. A few words, I hope don't disturb.

I'm just grateful meeting you even occurred.

It may be an understatement when I state that you blessed.
Your fate is success. You are Grace and Finesse.
When God Made You, He mixed Great with the Best.
Some women Probably hate how you shaped in a dress.
Your Brains are like Brilliance in a deep Treasure Chest.
& If you going East Baby I ain't Going West.
Life is a quest, less checkers, more chess.
And out of me you seem to bring the best.

Our future looks clear.
let me whisper in your ear.
This magic that's between us may it never disappear.
This magnet that's between us may it bring us more near.
your brains and your beauty make you so top tier

you curved like you're German engineered.
You learn and determined to persevere,

you perfect……
with purpose and career.
And really, I just like to have you near
You are the one that I will always revere.

I've been so busy today I didn't get a chance to write.

Couldn't wish YOU a good day but I wish YOU a good night.

I wish we were alike,

because when I see you, I get hype. This morning, I overslept and missed my sunny Delight.

Well I saw you in my sleep,

That's probably why it was deep.

you dumped me in the dream………and you called me cheap.

so, I robbed the bank for all the money and brought you a whole heap!

I kissed you on the cheek & told you it was yours to keep.

You said that made you weak

then gave me some of the best BLEEP BLEEP

then I held you, while we both fell asleep!!

I realized when you're around me and you start to get quiet,
your thoughts are probably loud as a riot
and I don't mean to incite it
but little lady you make me excited.
YOU'RE so Healthy
I need you in my diet...

When I awake in the morning,

You're the first mission.

Before I start my day and put my keys in the ignition.

I try to turn into an optician, and paint a picture so vivid, that maybe we can BOTH share this vision.

I really want to add, no division

and soon it'll be lemonade for any day you thought you caught a lemon.

In my dreams last night, I caught a vision.

Both of us were swimming, in a large race, and we were winning.

so, I took that as a sign to never treat you as the two.

I can have a threesome tonight but if them women not you. Then that's probably something that I wouldn't do.

I love you because you true

and on the real, you really worth a few.

I say that you're phenomenal, because you're my definition.

You helped me see clearly, in high definition.

Too many days without you and I'll definitely miss it.

Because every day you TFM, today's first mission.

In addition, I'll be dreaming about us working out and kissing

if you ever need my aid I will rush with assistance.

You keep me mindful to ALWAYS keep these hos at a distance.

I found your kind, AND

Over time I realized what I've been missing.

She knows that she's fire, she knows my desires

YOU'RE the future first lady of my empire.

You make my heart flip like clothes in a dryer,

and I don't want a taste, I want the whole entire.

This situation nice.

I want you situated for life.

You'll never have to lift a knife. I'll protect you with my life.

Haters throw salt,

At our wedding they'll throw rice.

If we stir it all together, we'll be seasoned real nice!!!

First lusts, then love. My feelings been sporadic.

Watching your beauty is like a movie, you been looking cinematic.

You should send me your picture, so the thought won't diminish.

You should have a photo shoot, you're the most photogenic.

Really baby? You ain't sent a photo in a minute.

You give to me, I give to you; I don't see no limits.

Loyalty overall,

We don't need the gimmicks.

And I promise to always uphold your image.

I wanna take a deep breath of you, probably with this intent,
that even if I lose you
I won't forget your scent.
Our foundation is cement...let's build a house not a tent.
Or maybe a multiplex that we can lease out and rent

If it makes dollars then YOU KNOW it makes sense
Your water is a blessing
I've been baptized and drenched.

I'm just preaching to the choir, giving tithes in the Pew
when I confess how I feel about you.
Yet and still, I do.
Because you make me feel brand new,
like everything you say to me is true.
Feeling like it's nothing I can't do.
Baby you give me courage with your wisdom and your strengths.
Your spirit calms me down till I feel less tense.
You graduate, I graduate to KING from a Prince
You my QUEEN and I won't stop till you convinced.

What you want for Christmas?

I don't ask for much, but I got you on my wish list.

The things you do ……make me do for you in an instant.

You gone be my wife cause you're too good to be my mistress.

Your mystique makes you sweeter than A Mistic.

Plus, you never nit pick

AND You're the only one I wanna get wit.

If you tried to weigh my love,

It probably breaks the scale.

You're a Disney vibe that came to life, a walking fairy tale.

From walking around our neighborhood, to exploring hidden trails.

To walking down an aisle, before we kiss, I lift your veil.

Am I under a spell??

 How we went from talking mail?

To me talking, trying to make you feel my words like Braille.

Your convo never stale, your brain sharp as a nail

plus, you Thick AS hell

girl I won't kiss and tell!!!!

Sexy Lady, you BE on my mind like all day...
Monday thru Sunday you sweet as a parfait…
Ever since I met you, I don't want you far away.
I want you by my side… when our hairs all grey.

When I Look into your eyes I get blinded by the light.
Beauty, Body and Brains, plus your aura sun bright.
I have seen a lot but, not another one like...
So when I do it for my Baby, I'll make sure it's done Right..

Brief moment of silence ..Girl you killem wit your shape.
If I had to Guess your flavor, I would say that it was Grape.
Cuz you fine like wine with your vintage kinda ways.
When I see you in the morning I have splendid Kind of days.
Thank you and I love you, what I tend to kinda say.
And

that's because I love you in an endless kinda way.

MY LADY!! my baby!! I hope you like the sound.
better yet be my queen, that's my wife with a crown.
I think about….. infinite… adjectives for my noun.
though she never says she likes me I can almost
hear the sound.
&
I'll repeat it
I'll be here anytime you need it.
Just tell me that you're hungry I won't hesitate to feed it.
Immediate!
this type of love ain't no intermediate.
my life is full of flavor lady, you the main
ingredient.

You'd be the answer if asked to define art,

the lay of your hair, the sway of your hind parts.

The way you say words, you define smart.

I want to readjust and align parts

and kiss you where your spine starts, or lick you where your spine ends.

Eat out for dinner, for dessert we should dine in,

any way you say it lady I'm in.

On a scale from 1 to 9 you are a divine 10.

I had a dream, I married you and your fine twin.

It was holy matrimony, it was love, it was trust.

Fire and desire both rubbed me with lust.

My alarm went off, I woke up in a rush,

threw my phone at the wall and told that mother ***** hush.

We're both one-of-a-kind
they can't mimic our design
when we sweat, you glisten, and I shine.
Rarely there's a time when she isn't on my mind.
Even through all the distance and the time.
We align.

ONCE I hurt my eyes, staring at your sunshine.
But don't mistake my kind for Blind.

I'm gonna give you rubies, diamonds and gold.
I want to give you love with my mind, heart and soul.
Your words warmed me up back when my heart was cold,
and we cut from a cloth that's extremely hard to fold!
You're so ladylike with the way that you behave,
and your courage through the roof, I can acknowledge that you're brave.
I know you'll never cave, I get chills when you wave.
Let's take the road less traveled on the road that we pave.

Listening to R&B I allowed my mind to wander…
I pondered, a platinum plaque for you, my favorite genre.
They say…. distance makes the heart grow fonder.
Mine grew like fields of marijuana.
That feeling that you give me, because I feel your persona,
and though I want it in the sun, I still want you in the sauna.
Its love, respect, and death before dishonor.
cause you my wife for life and all my babies Mamas.

It's real, all your skill and appeal is poetic.

Your vibrations give me energy that make me energetic.

Your beauty should be a course in the study of aesthetics.

You're magnetic & you don't need cosmetics.

You're the definition of excellence, priority, and precedence,

and that still don't describe what your essence is.

You're something much greater.

You move smooth like an ice skater.

your good mood gets me high as skyscrapers.

PLUS

you never hesitate to bring me down to earth…

I really dig how you so diverse.

Precious and priceless might best define your worth

let me skip who next in line…… I'm First.

It's power in your defiance, mixed with self-reliance,
We lions and this is small things to a giant.
Mind sharp as a razor with the speed of a laser…
This is a reminder! You Major!!
You already know the way, first you got to pray
then show your confidence in every word that you say.
I pray……, with all of the conviction I convey……
all our best attributes be on display.
Not just for today, but for life, until we both decay,
and I pray you let me join you on the way.

To be honest, I didn't know what I seen on the spot.

but now I know that you're the cream of the crop.

Thoughts about you never seeming to stop, I'm daydreaming a lot,

baby tell me, is we teaming or not?

You beam like water when it gleams off a yacht,

you like my favorite song I want to stream it a lot.

I want to show you off, like you seen what I got??

I hope you understand, I really mean what I jot.

I want you to promise me, you'll never let me go

wish I could read your mind but since I can't just let me know.

actions louder than words, so we should let it show.

how much we love each other over time... and let it grOW !

I hope you know I cherish every secret that you share with me.

time spent with you is like my therapy.

You provide clarity, I try to build you up cuz you're repairing me.

It's a must that I acknowledge your rarity.

You are prosperity,

Your love and your actions feel like charity.

If opposites attract this polarity.

Life is a gift, this is something like a present.

time is of the essence no better time than the present.

You are fine wine and your mind is effervescent.

life is full of lessons,

and yes, I confess it!

I haven't learned them all, but I recognize a blessing.

NO DOUBT

you are that, without a question.

I'm riding for you baby like equestrians & I'm

cheering for you lady,

go best friend!!!!

Hallelujah,

heavens what I see, when I see your face.

Your beauty is a picture I can't mimic nor trace.

I try to draw the picture but erase post haste

because few words seem worthy when I'm mentioning your grace.

Elegance, intelligence, you fly like Pelicans

with the strength to lead a Stampede of elephants

indeed, you are heaven sent

you make me walk tall like I'm SEVEN TEN

and I'ma take you places that you never been.

You my newest high like a new herb

You are simply superb, it's impossible to describe you in a few words.

When you step out in the morning, I hear Bluebirds

rejoicing at the very sight of you, and I know you heard.

You are glorious, victorious, hardworking, laborious.

You to Bonnie to my Clyde, we notorious.

African complexion so we warriors

Together we should pray, every day, and live our lives in euphoria.!!!

Do I love you for your old soul??

In them tights you look thicka than some grits in a cold bowl.

At times your beauty blinds me like diamonds on bold gold.

on the real you goals, goals!!

and the type I'd like to wife to make my soul whole.

Baby I hope you know that I ain't never switching up.
If I did it'd be to better me, to be a better me for us.
You make me so much better like what pie do for crust.
and I don't see no limits BOUT what I'll do for us.

Your Love and Respect Have to be earned this I learned.

Come and kiss my Lips, I'll lick your lips in return.

Memorize your Body Language, when it speaks, I can discern.

Believe your Love, Achieve your Love. Receive your Love in turn...

I haven't been this Happy with somebody in a while.

One day I'll put a body in your body, have my Child.

That's the second time I said that but baby it's no rush.

I say it so when we practice, it'll be more love making than lust.

I really need that the same way you need trust.

I'll always love you the same way that we discuss.

Having you in my life feels like a must.

Without you, its Disgust.

You better know, I   Love   US.

You are Infinity
you're Beauty & Divinity
Your Booty and Your Symmetry
plus all your Femininity.

It's the Best of Both Worlds Like Holy Water and Hennessey.

Your Energy is a Remedy, that Chemically
could NOT be made ACCIDENTALLY.
You're Brilliant Academically
You're Motion Picture Imagery

And I Love Being In Your Proximity.

When you Look AT me, do you see a chore?

I look At YOU and see a Beauty that I never seen before.

Like being stranded in the Ocean then I Finally see a shore.

I WANT to see her more, My Cherie Amour.

Sometimes when you wave, It's a Matrix Type of feel... I be thinking is she A.I.

Is this woman even Real?

That's why when you get close to me, I always try to feel.

Just to be sure you not a robot made of steel.

We went from crunch pallets
To lunch salads
To CONCH SALADS
Baby at this rate we can reach Trumps Palace
Anything is Possible
as long as we keep up progress.
I bring You Food Cuz You my Food and that shouldn't be hard to digest!!

Ever since I met you, the sky looks more beautiful.

I would argue you the greatest, but that fact is not disputable.

I would argue you the finest, but that fact is irrefutable.

I'll love you in ways that's uncommon and unusual.

I want you on me like a tattoo that's unremovable.

I can show you proof everything I say is provable.

Your Radiance is loud, its immutable,

and every time you walk it's a musical.

I hope the feelings mutual.

It's a feeling of gratification, when I use my imagination….
And dream this collaboration. Me and you could have the nation.
You're intoxication…No Exaggeration...
I did the math and tripled checked my calculations...
Right now, I'm making Calibrations.
Speaking out my affirmations………. In a love Language widely
known as patience
but When I see you I get anxious.
I tried not to say it and bury my feelings deep.
Lock it in a coffin and throw away the key... But it burst out like a zombie.
You probably view me as a creep.
Or some shoe smelling freak, that's always trying to speak.

Your Prestige is Prominent You allow me to be Dominant. Your Brilliance Demands Respect, and I honor it.

Sometimes I ponder this????????
If I could feed you compliments, that fill you up with confidence until
Our Love is consequent???
Or if, in your world......... I could be a continent??
With Resources and Monuments, and views of Astonishment???
If I could be your favorite meal, with all your favorite garnishes???
If Love is a Drug, you my favorite Pharmacist.

There you Have it!!!

35 Poems created to make the recipient of the message smile!!!!
Simply Put, there is power in making someone smile... An Authentic
Smile can break down walls and barriers, build trust and leave an
unforgettable impression. The moment you bring Joy into someone's
world you show them that they're seen, cherished and most importantly
valued.

Making someone smile can often improve your chances of building a
positive connection.

Creates a Positive Atmosphere: Smiling is associated with happiness
and comfort. If you make your love interest smile, you're creating a
moment of joy that they'll associate with you.

Breaks the Ice: Humor or lightheartedness can help ease tension,
making conversations more relaxed and enjoyable.

Shows Emotional Intelligence: The ability to make someone smile
demonstrates that you can read their emotions and respond in a way
that uplifts them.

Boosts Attraction: People are naturally drawn to those who make them
feel good. Making a person smile signals that you're fun, approachable,
and confident, qualities many find attractive.

Builds Connection: Sharing laughter or a smile creates a bond and shared experience, even if it's brief.

BUT the key is to be authentic and considerate. Forced humor or trying too hard can have the opposite effect. Focus on being genuine, attentive, and mindful of their sense of humor, and you'll EFFORTLESSLY improve your chances of leaving a positive impression.

Best of Luck. Peace and Blessings ..Til the next time.

Shefftal A. Baillou II

Disclaimer

This book and its poetry, as well as instructions should be used to BETTER your chances at Love.

The only Guarantee with this poetry is that each poem was written with Love. You are not guaranteed to make someone fall in love by sharing these poems. This poetry is for Art, and entertainment purposes.

This Book is designed to provide guidance and provoke inspiration, on your journey for personal growth and relationship success. While many of the outlined techniques have worked for countless people, **individual results may vary** and are decided by personal circumstances, efforts and many other personal factors. The Author and the Publisher make no guarantees of specific outcomes, including romantic success. For major relationship challenges or emotional challenges consider consulting a licensed professional.